LEVEL 2

# I'M BATGIRL!

Adapted by TRACEY WEST

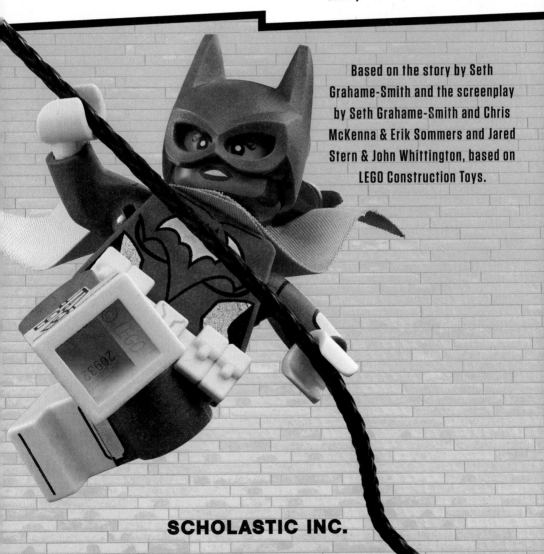

Based on the story by Seth Grahame-Smith and the screenplay by Seth Grahame-Smith and Chris McKenna & Erik Sommers and Jared Stern & John Whittington, based on LEGO Construction Toys.

SCHOLASTIC INC.

Based on the story by Seth Grahame-Smith and the screenplay by Seth Grahame-
Smith and Chris McKenna & Erik Sommers and Jared Stern & John Whittington, based
on LEGO Construction Toys.

All rights reserved. Published by Scholastic Inc., *Publishers since 1920.*
SCHOLASTIC and associated logos are trademarks and/or
registered trademarks of Scholastic Inc.

ISBN 978-1-338-11815-5

10 9 8 7 6 5 4 3 2 1               17 18 19 20 21

Printed in the U.S.A.                          40

First printing 2017

Book design by Jessica Meltzer

My name is Barbara Gordon. I'm the police commissioner of Gotham City. You might say I was born for the job. My dad, Jim Gordon, was commissioner for a long time.

My dad had help watching over Gotham City. Batman was always on call when he needed him. All my dad had to do was turn on the Bat-Signal.

But I looked up to my dad most of all. Growing up, I knew I wanted to be a police officer, just like him.

I was top of my class at Harvard for Police. Then I got a job in the town of Blüdhaven. I cleaned up the streets there. And I didn't need Batman to do it. Instead, I worked with my excellent team of police officers.

Then my dad retired. Gotham City offered me the job of police commissioner. My childhood dream had come true! I wanted the job. But I wasn't sure about one thing: Batman. I liked working on a team, and Batman wasn't exactly a team player.

The city held a big party for my dad's retirement.

That night, at the party, I gave a speech.

"Look, Batman's been on the job for a very, very, very, very long time," I said. "However, in spite of having a full-time Batman, Gotham City is still the most crime-ridden city in the world."

People in the crowd started to mumble. I knew they agreed with me. But billionaire Bruce Wayne argued with me.

"What's your problem with Batman?" he asked. "What did Batman do to you?"

"I'm not a Batman hater," I replied. "But we don't need an unsupervised, adult man in a Halloween costume karate-chopping our citizens left and right. What I want is to partner with Batman."

"No!" Bruce exclaimed.

"Wouldn't that be better?" I asked. "I'm sure Batman could use the help."

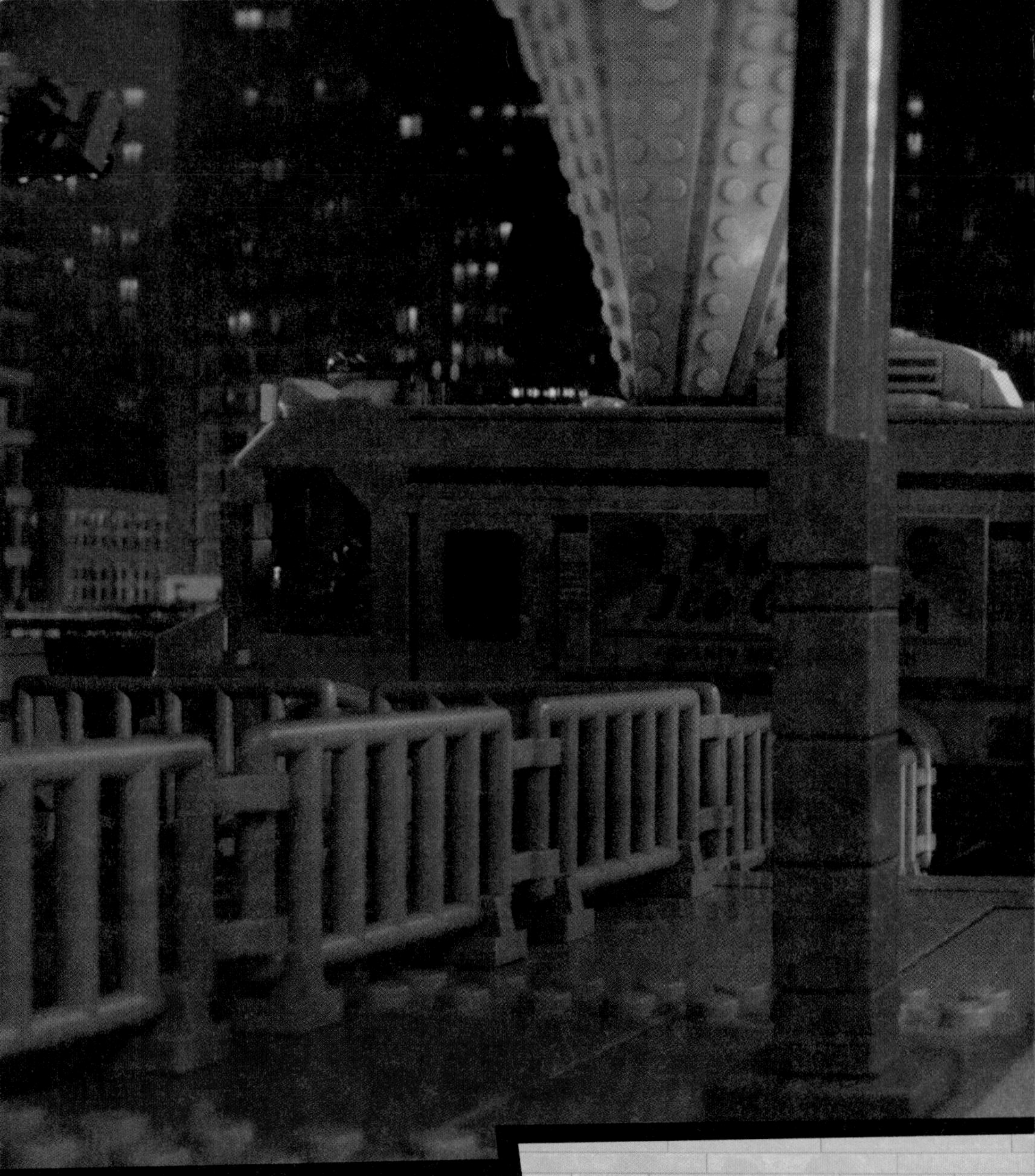

I was about to finish my speech when a bunch of ice cream trucks pulled up all around the gala. The doors opened and bad guys started pouring out. I knew those clowns were trouble.

"Everybody get down!" I yelled.

The Joker showed up, followed by the rest of
Gotham City's super-villains.

I ran toward the Joker, ready to face him. But who
do you think came between us? You guessed it.
Batman!

"Oh, Batman's here!" the Joker said. "Wonderful! I've got a surprise for you guys, and it's going to make you smile. I . . . surrender!"

I was surprised. So was Batman. Even the super-villains looked surprised.

But it was no joke. Joker calmly walked into the back of a police car.

"Joker, you have the right to remain silent," I told him.

"Okay!" said Joker cheerfully.

But Batman was suspicious of the Joker. He looked at me.

"And you have the right to chill out for one second because the Joker is not surrendering to you!" he insisted.

"We can question him together, okay?" I asked.

But that wasn't okay with Batman. "Look, the Joker wants to go to Arkham Asylum," he said. "That's the last place *any* criminal wants to go. Unless—*ding ding ding!*—he's got some big plan."

"What if you put him in the Phantom Zone?" somebody in the crowd called out.

"The Phantom Zone! That's a great idea," Batman said.

He tried to pull the Joker out of the police car, but I had my officers stop him. Once again, Batman was trying to do things by himself. And we needed to work together.

We rounded up all the super-villains and locked them in Arkham Asylum with the Joker. All but one. I noticed that Harley Quinn was missing. So I called Batman to let him know. I hoped we could work together to find her.

But Batman wasn't interested in working together. He showed up at Arkham Asylum with some kid in a costume and a Phantom Zone Projector. Then he blasted the Joker into the Phantom Zone!

I was tired of Batman taking things into his own hands. I locked him in a cell.

We quickly learned that Batman was right. The Joker's surrender was a trap—just not the trap Batman expected. Harley Quinn grabbed the Phantom Zone Projector and used it to open up the Phantom Zone.

The Phantom Zone hovered above the city. Then the Joker's face appeared all over Gotham City.

"I could never take over the city with all the old loser villains," the Joker said. "So I've collected some new Gotham City friends to help out!"

The Joker and his new evil friends started causing trouble right away! I knew I needed Batman's help with this. But I really needed him to work as a team this time.

"I don't need anyone's help," Batman said firmly.

I wanted to leave Batman in his cell when he said that.

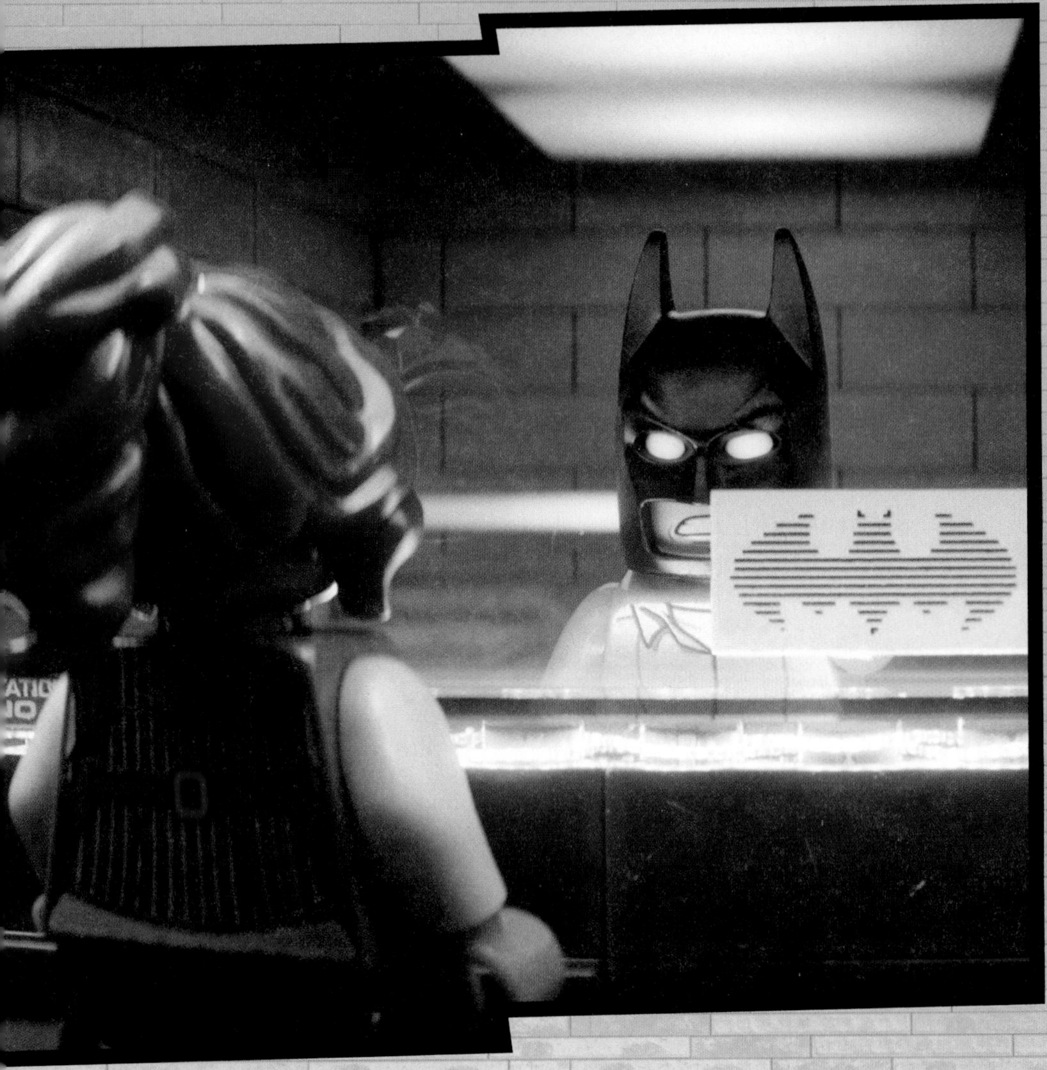

But there was a kid there, along with Bruce Wayne's butler, Alfred. The kid convinced Batman to help us.

I let him out of jail. "But you have to promise you'll team up with me until the end," I warned him.

"I promise for sure," Batman said. "I'll do whatever it takes to stop the Joker. Even if it means working as a team. Let's go!"

"Now, Barbara, you are officially representing the Batman brand," he told me. "That means you have to use officially licensed gadgets."

Batman started shooting stuff out of his merch gun.

*Kaboom!* He shot out a costume for Alfred.

He shot out a bunch of Bat-gadgets for the kid and me, too.

Now we were a real crime-fighting team!

We left Arkham Asylum. The Joker and his evil friends had taken over the streets of Gotham City. I tried to lead the team to safety.

"Okay, follow me. I'll be on point," I told the others. "Batman, you're my cover. Robin, Alfred, you're lookouts."

But Batman didn't follow me. He ran right past me!

"Batman, what are you doing?" I asked.

"I'm following ahead of you," he replied.

"The phrase is following *behind* you," I said.

I quickly figured out that Batman was lying when he said he wanted to work as a team. All my cool Bat-gadgets were made of chocolate, useless against the bad guys. But he wouldn't share his tools.

And when he built us a Batwing, it only had room for one! We had to cram in there.

Scary bad guys were taking over the city! Batman had no choice. He had to let us help him. Together, Batman, Alfred, Robin, and I took down some big baddies.

But we still needed to capture the Joker. Batman wanted to do it all by himself. So he locked me, Alfred, and Robin into the Batwing.

He left us, and the Joker's evil friends attacked the Batwing. Robin escaped and ran to find Batman. Then Alfred and I escaped. But the bad guys captured Robin!

That's about when Batman showed up.

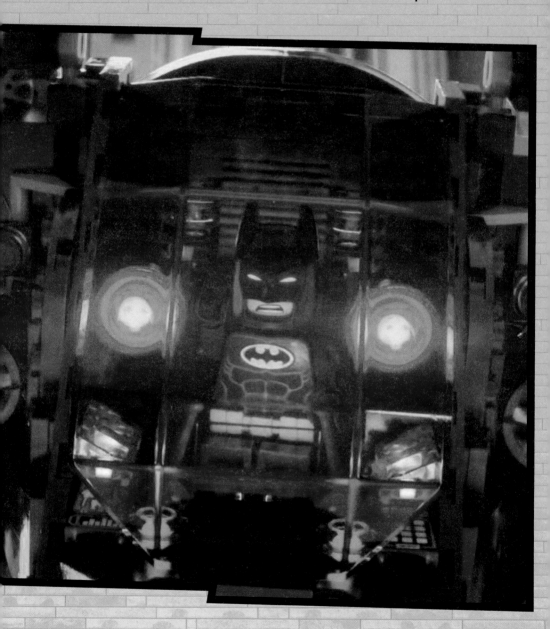

I was angry with Batman. I started to walk away.

"Barbara, please don't leave," he said.

I stopped. "Why?" I asked.

"Because there's something I need to say to you," he replied. "Click."

I frowned. "Click? Click doesn't mean anything, Batman," I said.

"Sorry, you've got to turn around," Batman told me.

I turned around. The Bat-Signal flashed in the night sky. But it was different.

It looked like me.

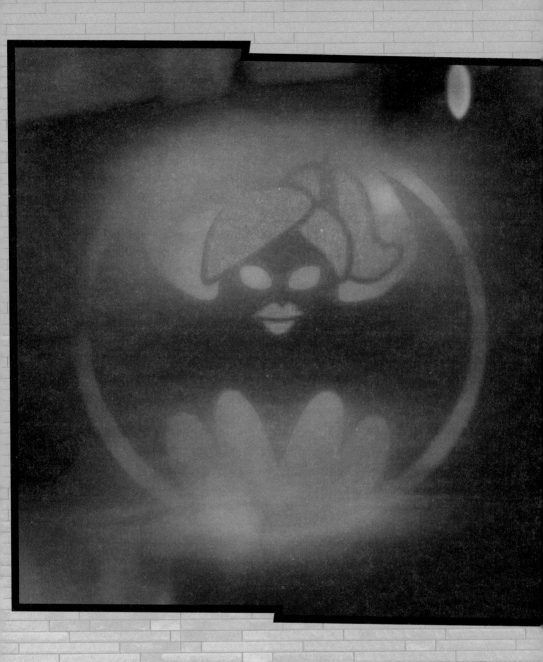

"I call it the Babs-signal," Batman said. "And I'm flipping the switch for you because I really need your help, Barbara. I really, really do. What do you say, commissioner? Will you work with me?"

I shook his hand. "Always," I said.

We still had bad guys to fight. And Robin to save. And the Joker to catch. But from that moment on, I was part of Batman's team.

I was Batgirl!

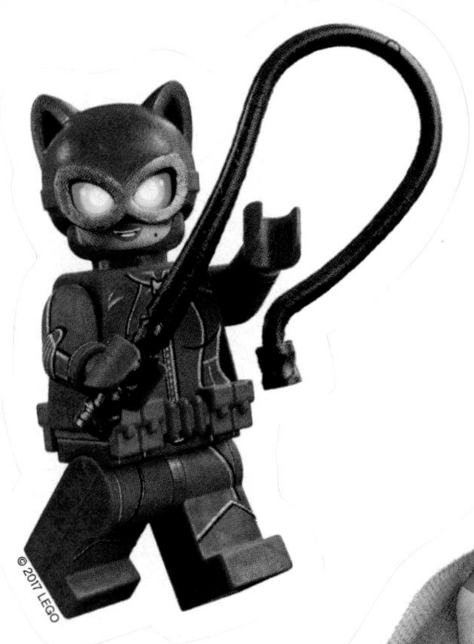
© 2017 LEGO

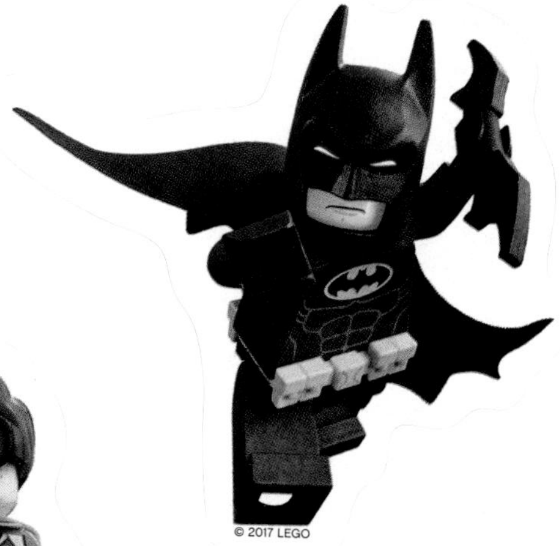
© 2017 LEGO

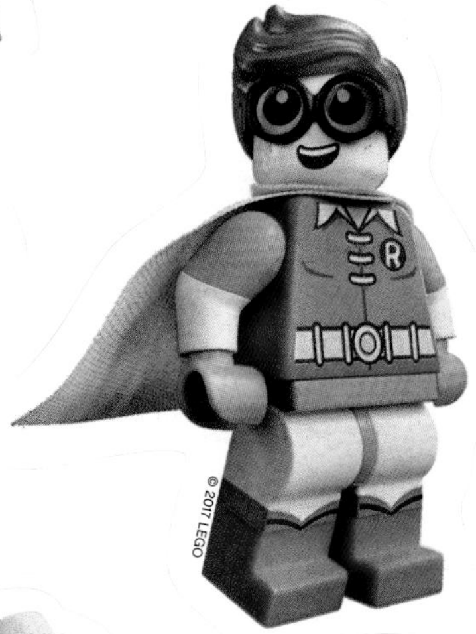
© 2017 LEGO

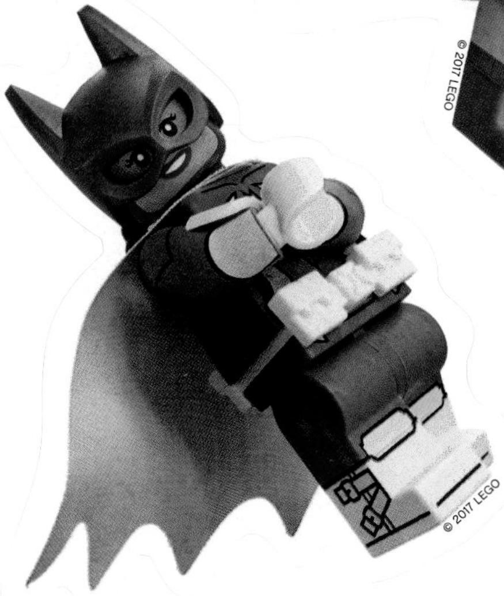
© 2017 LEGO

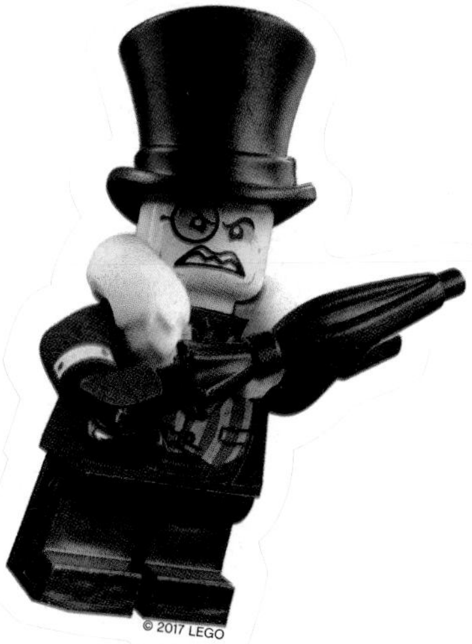
© 2017 LEGO

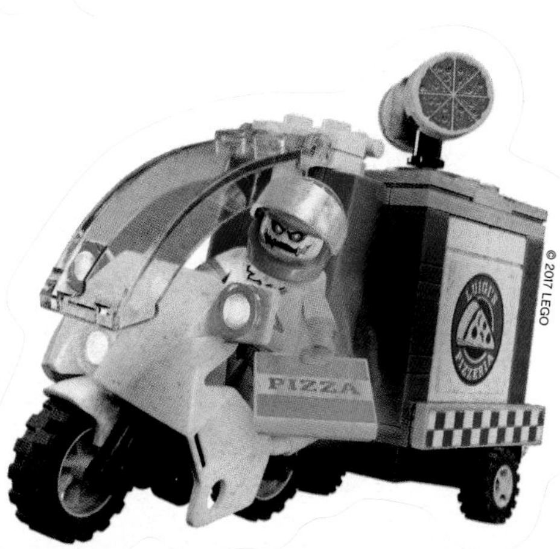
PIZZA
© 2017 LEGO

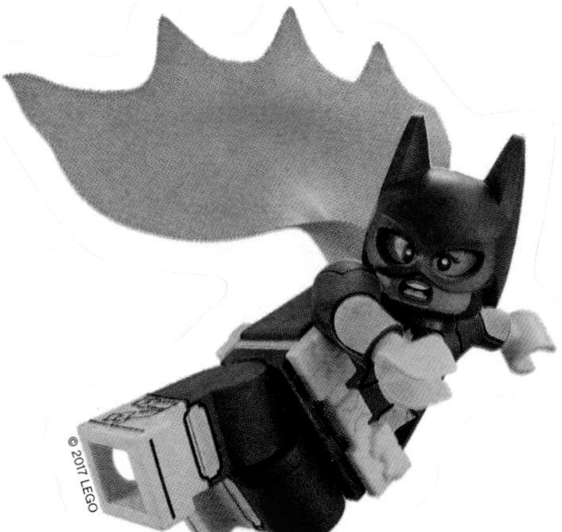
© 2017 LEGO


ISBN 978-1-338-11815-5 PO# 546271